The
Gaping Wide~Mouthed
Waddling Frog

HISTORICAL NOTE

The Gaping Wide-mouthed Waddling Frog first appeared about 1822 and was used as a memory game. The rules of the game are that the first player holds up some small object and says to the second player, "Take this". The second player takes the object and asks, "What's this?" The first player answers, "A gaping wide-mouthed waddling frog". The second player then addresses the third player, "Take this" and so on until each player has had a turn. On the second round, the players answer the "What's this?" question with, "Two pudding ends that won't choke a dog, nor a gaping wide-mouthed waddling frog" and so on, with each round being longer and harder to remember.

The Gaping Wide~Mouthed Waddling Frog

a counting book

illustrated by
RODNEY McRAE

PICTURE CORGI BOOKS

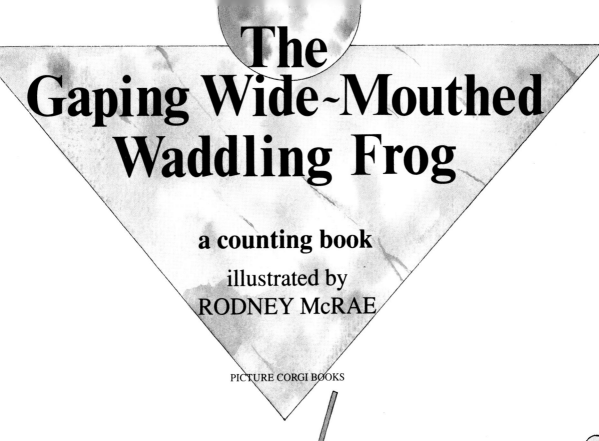

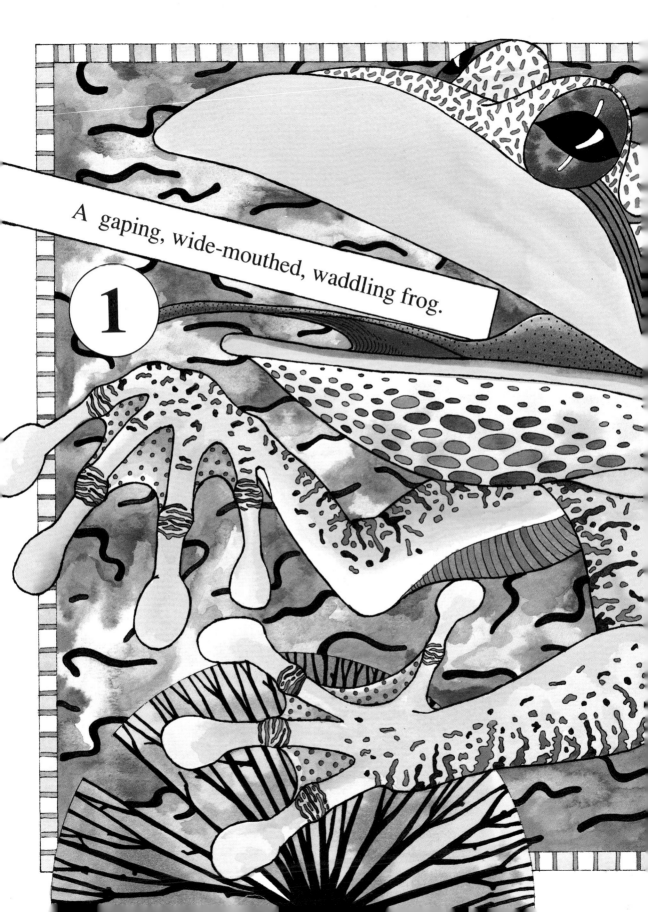

1

A gaping, wide-mouthed, waddling frog.

2

TWO pudding ends that won't choke a dog,

Nor a gaping, wide-mouthed, waddling frog.

THREE monkeys tied to a log,

3

FOUR horses stuck in a bog,

4

5

FIVE puppies by our dog Ball,

That daily for their breakfast call;

SIX beetles against the wall,

6

Close to an old woman's apple stall;

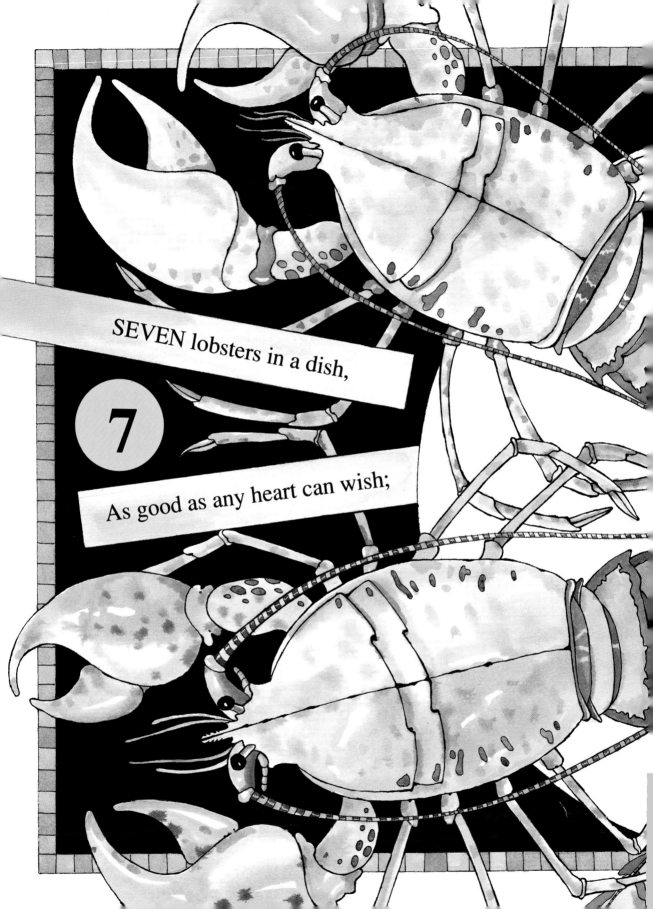

7

SEVEN lobsters in a dish,

As good as any heart can wish;

EIGHT joiners in Joiners' Hall,

Working with their tools and all;

8

NINE peacocks in the air,

9

I wonder how they all got there,

You don't know, and I don't care;

10

TEN comets in the sky,

Some low and some high;

ELEVEN ships sailing on the main,
Some bound for France, and some for Spain,

11

I wish them all safe back again;

TWELVE huntsmen with horns and hounds,
Hunting over other men's grounds;

12

TWELVE huntsmen with horns and hounds,

ELEVEN ships sailing on the main,

TEN comets in the sky,

NINE peacocks in the air,

EIGHT joiners in Joiners' Hall,

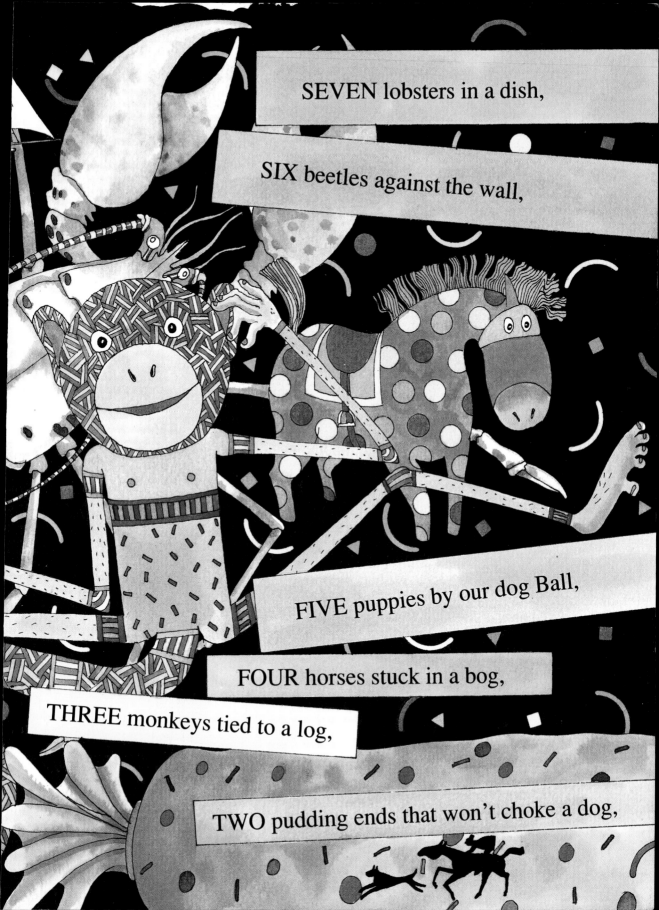

SEVEN lobsters in a dish,

SIX beetles against the wall,

FIVE puppies by our dog Ball,

FOUR horses stuck in a bog,

THREE monkeys tied to a log,

TWO pudding ends that won't choke a dog,

Nor a gaping, wide-mouthed, waddling frog.

Twelve huntsmen with horns and hounds,
Hunting over other men's grounds;
Eleven ships sailing on the main,
Some bound for France, and some for Spain,
I wish them all safe back again;
Ten comets in the sky,
Some low and some high;
Nine peacocks in the air,
I wonder how they all got there,
You don't know, and I don't care;
Eight joiners in Joiners' Hall,
Working with their tools and all;
Seven lobsters in a dish,
As good as any heart can wish;
Six beetles against a wall,
Close to an old woman's apple stall;
Five puppies by our dog Ball,
Who daily for their breakfast call;
Four horses stuck in a bog,
Three monkeys tied to a log,
Two pudding ends that won't choke a dog,

NOR A GAPING WIDE-MOUTHED WADDLING FROG!

THE GAPING WIDE-MOUTHED WADDLING FROG
A PICTURE CORGI 0 552 525839

PRINTING HISTORY
First publication in Great Britain 1989
Published simultaneously by Dell, a division of Transworld Publishers
(Australia) Pty Ltd, 1989
Originated and developed by Margaret Hamilton Books Pty Ltd

Picture Corgi Books are published by Transworld Publishers Ltd.,
61-63 Uxbridge Road, Ealing, London W5 5SA.

Made and printed in Singapore by Kyodo-Shing Loong Printing
Industries Pte Ltd